THE BONE
MAIDEN

an IMMORTAL WAKE PREQUEL NOVELLA
ZACHRY WHEELER

eBook ISBN: 978-1-954153-05-9
Paperback ISBN: 978-1-954153-06-6
Edited by Jennifer Amon
Published by Mayhematic Press

This story is Eric's fault.

CHAPTER 1

The Great Onslaught of 2048 marked the end of mortal rule. In 2136, the vampires united to give birth to the Eternal Age. The years in between became known as the Savage Gap, a period of violent anarchy that decimated the remaining population. Humans were hunted to the brink of extinction. Desperate to survive, they turned to espionage to regain control.

The humans feared the hunters.

The hunters feared the spies.

But when darkness fell, everyone feared the Bone Maiden.

* * *

The sun was setting over the mountains of southern Colorado. The fall months brought a mosaic of color to the landscape. The air was pleasantly cool, but not cold enough to keep hunters out of the area. The ruins of Durango, an old retirement town, stood as a hollow reminder of a bygone era. Plants had reclaimed the pavement. Buildings had fallen into decay. The charred husks of unfought fires lingered as monuments of neglect.

The town was dead.

And the population that once called it home was likely dead too.

Aspen trees cast long shadows across an abandoned roadway. They stretched and whined as strong winds swept over the canopy. The creaking of their trunks echoed through the valley, serving as the only vocal presence for miles on end.

A shadow departed from the mass and raced across the road. His rubber soles tapped across the dirty pavement. When he reached the other side, he turned to inspect his path. He scanned for any obvious prints, but the wind had already erased the evidence. His tattered clothes fluttered in the breeze as he scanned the decaying strip mall on the other side. Coffee shop, pet store, and the remains of a plundered pharmacy. He sighed, then turned and continued his trek towards an old gas station.

The man crossed the embankment and passed under a broken billboard on his way to the front entrance. He stepped over fueling hoses lying on the concrete, long since drained of their precious bounties. When he reached the doorless entry, he gave the vicinity one final scan before disappearing inside.

The interior was dank and sullied, reclaimed by the elements it once banished. Anything worth eating had rotted away. Anything worth using had been taken. The man walked by rusted shelves without a second glance, certain that he would find nothing of value. A small alcove at the rear housed two doors, one to a public toilet and the other to a storage room. He reached for the latter and pulled the handle with a gentle grip, careful not to make any noise. The dim glow of candlelight crept into the alcove. He glanced over his shoulder, then slipped inside and closed the door behind him.

When the door latched, he turned to find a middle-aged woman and a preteen girl huddled in the corner. His wife and daughter. A pair of stumpy candles rested on an overturned bucket. The flames illuminated the cramped interior, no bigger than a generous closet and long emptied of its worth. The woman, also wrapped in frayed attire, met eyes with the man and asked the pressing question without saying a word.

The man frowned and shook his head.

2

The woman closed her eyes and released a heavy sigh.

The daughter, having read the room, offered some assurance. "I can make it until morning," she said. "Promise."

As if on cue, the girl started coughing violently. The mother provided comfort as the man winced at every hack. The girl pressed her face into her mother's chest, muffling the coughs as best she could. The mother whispered soothing words into her ear, then lifted an anxious gaze to the man. He mirrored her distress. When the coughing stopped, the mother released her grip and leaned the girl against the wall. She patted her daughter's dusty cheek before standing to confer with her husband. They gathered in the opposite corner.

"We have some ibuprofen in the cave," the woman said with a near-whisper.

The man shook his head. "We can't make it. We're here for the night."

"Was there anything else in the pharmacy? Pain meds, aspirin, anything?"

"No. Wiped clean."

The woman sighed and bowed her head.

The girl coughed again, causing both parents to flinch.

"Maybe we can make it," the man said with a hesitant tone.

"We can't risk taking her outside. One cough and they—" The woman groaned and thought for a moment. "What about elderberries? An old remedy, but they work."

The man lifted his ratty sleeve, revealing a tarnished Rolex with a cracked face. "Twenty minutes until sunset. I can try, maybe stay out longer if needed."

"There are hunters in the area. We heard them two nights back."

"North of town. We're in the lower valley."

The woman sneered.

"I know," the man said, adding a sigh.

"And what about *her*?"

The man grimaced and glanced away.

"Don't you dare dismiss it," the woman said with a harsh whisper. "She was spotted in the area two weeks ago."

"Allegedly."

"Alleg—you saw the markings."

"The scribblings of a madman for all we know. I fear hunters, not myths."

"The Bone Maiden is not a myth. You know that. We've seen the—" She paused to choose the word. "The *remnants*, with our own eyes."

"It's the hyoid bone, right?" the daughter said before releasing another cough.

Both parents turned to her.

"She rips it from the throats of her victims. If it's human, she keeps it. She adds it to a trophy bag that she carries like a sack of coins. But if it's from one of *them*, she clutches it inside her fist until it dissolves."

The parents traded uneasy glances.

"Where did you hear that?" the man said to his daughter.

"From Nathan. Just before he, um ..." She looked away.

The woman patted the man's shoulder, signaling him to depart.

"Back soon," he said, then vanished behind the door.

The mother took a deep breath, then stepped over to the girl and settled beside her. A malaise infected the room. Candles flickered, pulsing shadows across the walls. The mother searched for words as the daughter stared into the darkness beyond.

"You know," the mother said, opting for a softer tone, "your father may be right. Many think that the maiden doesn't exist. Some say she's a parable, an apparition dreamed up to keep us on our toes."

"Complacency is death," the girl said with mild annoyance. The family motto, the maxim of all humanity, was etched into her very existence.

The mother smiled. "Exactly."

"But there are so many stories."

"Every faith has stories. They're used to teach, to guide, t—"

"To frighten."

The mother nodded slowly. "That too." She glanced at the door and swallowed a whimper, desperate to relieve the dread coursing through her body.

*　*　*

The man glanced back at the gas station as he pushed towards the forest line nearby. The sun hovered above the mountains, now a dull orange orb inching towards the crest. He frowned at the image, one that he hadn't seen for quite some time. A sudden rush of urgency snapped his gaze back to the trees. He leapt into a jog through the tall grass, fast enough to save precious seconds, but slow enough to keep his presence hidden.

Sound remained the biggest threat out in the open, and a soft gait remained the best defense. Howling winds swept through the valley, gifting the man some audible cover. It was a welcome bonus, but far from assurance given their heightened senses. One wrong step could be his last, so he studied his path carefully while scanning the periphery.

White flowers, he thought, the telltale sign of an elderberry bush. They were out of season, but some wild growth should remain. Before long, he had traveled half a mile from the station, hugging the tree line to maximize visibility. Sunlight waned minute by minute, reducing his chances while increasing the panic.

And then he saw it.

White flowers beside a large tree.

An elderberry bush.

A small one, but a victory nonetheless. A grunt of relief crawled up his throat, but he forced it back to the silent abyss. With no time to lose, the man rushed over to the bush and dropped to his knees. He plucked a small cloth bag from his pocket and teased it open. Eager hands reached for the tiny black berries, but stopped before plucking the first bunch.

Calm yourself.

His widened gaze raked across the valley. Rotting houses stood as grim reminders. Rusted cars dotted the nearby roadway. And most frightening of all, a final sliver of sunlight vanished behind the mountain. The muted hues of dusk painted the valley. But mercifully, no movement accompanied them.

The man spun back to the bush and plucked as many berries as he could. The bounty was small, but the sack filled quickly. He cinched it shut and tied it to his belt. The dimming light prodded his nerves, but time remained on his side. Most activity resumed an hour after sunset. *Gray time*, he thought. Dangerous, but not dire.

He climbed to his feet, double-checked the sack, then panned his gaze across the valley before proceeding. Rotting houses, rusted cars, and a shadowy figure standing in the roadway.

The man froze and held his breath.

Every muscle seized inside his body.

The growing darkness shrouded the figure. Be it facing or turned away, the man could not tell. But a standoff commenced nonetheless. He stood beside the trees as a tree himself, hoping that his presence remained unseen.

The figure stood about 50 yards away.

Not enough, the man thought.

Certain death in a chase.

The forest, he thought. *Hope lies in the forest.*

Every second an eternity.

And then the figure stepped forward.

Towards the man.

One step became two.

Two became three.

And three became a sprint.

The man spun and scurried into the forest. Leaves crunched beneath his feet as panicked breaths fled his lungs. A guttural growl echoed behind him, followed by another not far away. Two hunters began their pursuit. The man plowed through brush and sailed around trees, using every ounce of adrenaline to maintain distance. The darkness deepened, blurring the vision he so desperately needed. Dim outlines provided anchors, but only for a few short minutes. He crashed through branches and kicked rocks, gifting his pursuers everything they needed.

The growls grew louder.

Dread swelled in the man's chest, but he pushed on.

Louder.

The man peered over his shoulder, catching nothing more than fractured shadows. When he turned back, a thick branch bashed his face and yanked him off his feet. His back slammed into the dirt, forcing a yelp from his chest. The taste of blood was immediate, but fear kept his body in motion.

The fight had come.

The man plucked a knife from his boot and scrambled behind the nearest tree. Returning to his feet, he flipped the blade and cocked his elbow, hoping to catch the first hunter by surprise. His heart thumped furiously as he fought to muffle his panting.

The growls grew louder.

I fight so they can live, the man thought.

Louder.

So they can live.

As the man tensed for a strike, the growl morphed into a shriek. A heavy thump tremored through the dirt. Hisses turned to gurgles, then fell silent. A second growl followed, but met a similar fate after a brief struggle. Peace returned to the forest. Gusts of wind rushed over the canopy, rustling leaves and creaking branches.

The man dared not peek.

He remained pressed to the tree, frozen and hidden. His breathing slowed to a muted pant. His muscles trembled, still poised to strike. A cut along his cheek trickled blood into his mouth. The voiceless aftermath goaded his mind, urging him to seek closure.

And so he peered around the tree.

There, lying in the dirt, were the mangled bodies of two hunters. Deep gashes continued to spill blood into black pools. One head was severed and the other nearly so. The smell of sweat and iron teased his nostrils, masking the floral sweetness of the forest. A bear, perhaps. A silly notion, but the only rationality his mind could muster.

That is, until he turned around.

A hooded figure stood before him, mere feet away.

The sudden fright unlocked his grip and the knife fell to the ground. He glanced down as the last flickers of twilight reflected off the blade. A weighted sigh escaped his chest, for his fate no longer belonged to him.

So they can live, he thought.

The figure did not move, allowing the man to slowly scan its profile. Sturdy leather, satchel, looped belt with several pouches. Ungloved hands, feminine, one of which was soaked in blood and clutching an unseen object.

"You should forage east," the figure said.

The man faltered. "Are you ... *her?*"

"There's a hunting party six miles to the south. You should forage east."

The man glanced around the forest, then returned his gaze to the figure. "How do you know?"

"Longevity lifts all veils."

The man huffed. "So it's true. You're one of *them*."

"Them. Us. It's all the same."

"Then why spare me? Why kill your own?"

"Because they hunt for the wrong reasons." She pointed to the sack tied to his belt, now stained by crushed berries. "You do not."

Relief flooded his body, allowing his stance to soften. His glistening eyes screamed with gratitude as he fought the urge to weep.

"East," the maiden said, then turned to leave.

"What will you do, then?" the man said as she walked away.

"Hunt the hunters." She rounded a thicket and disappeared.

CHAPTER 2

A full moon had replaced the sun over Durango, blanketing the abandoned suburbs with dim light. Vines slithered around old streetlamps. The sidewalks beneath them had long disappeared, swallowed by decorative greenery once hacked by trimmers and mowers. Mailboxes rose above the tall grass, devoid of purpose, but sturdy enough to serve as grave markers.

The cracked concrete of a cul-de-sac formed a wide circle around a burly man. He stood at the center, glaring up at the moon as if to chastise an intruder. The reflected light revealed his true face, a leathery mask with sharp brows and a scruffy beard. His brawny frame was wrapped in a thick black cloak, creating the image of a hardened marauder.

The faint taps of approaching footsteps caught his attention, but not enough to startle. They were familiar to his ears. He snarled at the moon one last time and turned to find a slender man taking his final steps. The frayed sash around his neck fluttered in the evening breeze. His frame was paltry by comparison, but carried the same hardened exterior.

"Anything?" the brute said with a gruff voice.

"No," the slender man said, his tone flat and dismissive. "No signs, no scents, even the ashes are old and caked." He glanced back at the rotting McMansion that he had scoured. "And even if there were spies around, they wouldn't be holed up here. This is all quick-build trash. Haven't seen a bunker or basement since we left town."

The brute grunted.

"I say we skip the rest and find a wild meal."

The brute sighed, then glanced at the moon and nodded. "Agreed." His eyes lowered to the street and panned around the houses. "Where's Kendra?"

One of the front doors creaked open, drawing their gazes. A lone figure emerged from within and paused to rest against the frame.

"We're calling it," the brute said, loud enough to echo down the empty street.

The figure did not respond. It lifted off the frame and began a limp shuffle towards the men, like a drunk searching for a place to crash.

The slender man chuckled. "Find some whiskey?"

"And did you save some for us?" the brute said.

The figure passed beneath an oak tree and into the moonlight, revealing her dirty blonde hair and rugged clothes. Her slumped posture and dangling arms gave her a zombie-like gait. As she neared the men, her gasping breaths became apparent.

The grin faded from the brute's face. "What's wrong?"

No response.

"Look," the slender man said. He pointed to a trail of black behind the woman. It glistened beneath the moonlight, an oil-like substance that snaked back to the house. It also trickled from her mouth and dripped from her crooked knuckles.

Blood.

As Kendra stepped onto the pavement, her crippled body surrendered. She fell to her knees and landed on her chest, revealing the multiple stab wounds covering her back. The deep gashes had stained her tunic black and poured blood down her legs.

The brute raced over to help, but quickly realized that the only footsteps were his own. His gaze whipped back to the slender man, who stood petrified in the grip of a hooded figure. One hand covered his mouth while the other pressed the blade of a machete to the back of his neck. The slender man wheezed with fright, his arms open wide and pleading for mercy. The hooded figure maintained its calm and disarming leverage. Its feet were firmly planted, and a forearm steadied the blade from handle to tip.

Every muscle seized inside the brute's body as he realized what stood before him. His breathing quickened. A million pleas flooded his mind. The violence that came so naturally had abandoned him. He was staring into the void and only his wits would save him. But as he opened his mouth to speak, fate declared its true intention.

"Run, little piggy," the maiden said, then drove the blade through the slender man's neck.

The brute stumbled back and leapt into a sprint as the headless body of his cohort crumpled to the ground. A surge of adrenaline pushed him past driveways and mailboxes, his heavy boots clomping down the avenue like mallets on stone. He rounded a corner and down another street, allowing him to peer back at the cul-de-sac.

The maiden stood her ground.

She loomed over her victim as a dark pool crept around her feet. The machete blade hung from her grip, pulling the moonlight into its newly black sheen. She taunted the brute from afar, like a hungry cheetah stalking a gazelle. With a practiced hand, she reached down to the bloody stump and ripped her prize from the flesh. She glared at the fleeing brute, then vanished into the shadows.

The brute returned his full focus to the street. He pressed forward with every ounce of energy, desperate to outrun the apparition. As he rounded another corner, he found himself disoriented, trapped inside a maze with no clue how to escape. He skidded to a halt at an intersection and spun around to gather his bearings.

Every shadow a monster.

Every sound a deafening conclusion.

The moon outlined a familiar mountain in the distance. His widened eyes locked onto the peak, restoring his orientation. But as he leaned forward to proceed, a sharp clank needled his ear. Metal on bone, a sound he knew all-too-well.

And then came the pain.

And then his legs departed.

He fell to the pavement, paralyzed and helpless, for the maiden had severed his spine with a swipe to the lower back. She towered over him with blood still dripping from the blade, but the brute remained facedown and dared not meet her eye. The pain would be temporary. He knew that. One of the many unearned gifts of immortality. But the time that he so brazenly took for granted was no longer on his side. He panted and sweated, fists pressed to the concrete, gritting his teeth as he awaited the fatal blow.

True death.

But it never came.

The pain remained, and he found himself getting used to it. The sensation was sharp yet familiar, as the life of a hunter was hard and brutal. Panic slowly morphed into curiosity. He twisted his gaze to the side, revealing the maiden sitting on the pavement several feet away. Her legs were crossed with hands folded in her lap. She seemed pensive, as if seeking permission to end the session. Moonlight revealed the flesh within. Round chin, soft cheeks, strands of long hair tucked into the hood. She reserved a feminine allure, despite the terror she inflicted.

The brute stared at her, captivated, but loath to speak.

"The strike was clean," she said, her tone neutral and detached. "Lumbar disc. Four days to heal, should I permit it."

The brute coughed a dollop of blood onto the pavement. He sighed, yielding to the deadfall that besieged him. "Speak your peace, then."

"Where is Sala Rain?"

He grunted into a throaty chuckle. "Ah, I see. Having trouble finding your precious mark?"

"So you know him."

"Yes, but he hasn't hunted in years."

"What do you mean?"

"He's an agent now—*cough*. Hand of Malin."

"Malin. You mean *warlord* Malin?"

"The very same. He's in Denver recruiting sub-factions."

"That's suicide. NWS controls everything west of the Mississippi."

"Not to battle—*cough*. To shore up power for the coming union."

The maiden paused. "Union?"

The brute rolled onto his side and propped on an elbow. He sneered at the maiden, as if shielded by a riddle. "You've been away too long."

"Tell me everything."

"No," the man said bluntly. "Unlike you, I'm not a traitor to the new world."

She lifted the machete and pressed the tip to his chest.

He smirked in defiance, goading her to do what he knew she could not. "The game has shifted, I see."

The maiden thought for a moment, then returned the machete to her side. A grim silence settled between them. Their gazes locked. The brute maintained his hardened stare while the maiden peered beyond him.

"A few years after the Great Onslaught," she said, "I was tracking some raiders through the Florida panhandle. I caught up to them as they were attacking a survivor settlement. Most were dead when I arrived, and the raiders were busy feasting. As I stalked the perimeter, I stumbled across a raider trying to rape a villager. Young girl, barely a teen. He had pinned her to the dirt and was fumbling at his belt. She was screaming, punching, fighting for life. But what could she do? The vamp was too strong. The outcome was inevitable. And yet she fought. It was strangely poetic, like a fly struggling against the paper."

She tightened her grip around the machete handle. "But the fly is just a fly, and the paper exists to torment. So when he reared back for leverage, I rushed in and split him in half below the chest. My blade cut through two elbows and a torso. This blade, in fact. Well, not *this* blade. I have replaced it many times. Bone tends to dull the steel, you see. Anyway, the top half thumped into the grass while the bottom half bathed the girl in blood. Her screams stopped, as if washed away by a wrathful baptism. The head and chest writhed on the ground as an armless abomination. Blood gurgled from every hole. It seemed like an appropriate fate, so I helped the girl escape and left the rapist to die."

The maiden leaned forward, as if to relay a secret. "But here's the thing. I returned several days later to resume the hunt. And much to my surprise, the rapist was still alive. He had crawled into a nearby shed, using his stumps to push along. He was weak and pale, alone and abandoned, but *alive*. His lower half had dissolved, but his upper half had scarred over and started to heal. It was strangely captivating, like a severed tail twitching in the dirt."

The brute shifted his widened eyes.

"Kill the brain, kill the beast. We all know that. Stab it, crush it, remove the head, doesn't matter. It all results in ash. So why did half a ribcage make a difference?"

The maiden allowed the question to linger. Her fingertips rapped the machete blade, taunting the brute with rumination.

"And so, I did what any curious girl would do. I dissected the rapist piece by piece, making damn sure that his final moments were spent in howling agony. I removed both arm stumps. Nothing. I removed his ribs, his shoulders, his eyes, even his lower jaw to muffle the screams. But nothing I did triggered the fatal reaction.

"That is, until I removed the heart.

"Not gently, of course. I ripped it from his chest like pulling a weed from the earth. But that was it. Soon thereafter, I watched his mangled face crumble into ash."

The brute swallowed a whimper as the maiden lifted her fist between them. The blood that once stained her grip had vanished. Her fingers fanned open, releasing a puff of ash into the evening breeze. Forever silent was the slender man.

"So you have a choice," she said with a ghoulish tone. "Tell me everything. Here. Now. Or I will carry your butchered flesh until you do."

Loyalty grew heavy inside the brute's chest. His eyelids fell, for the acceptance of reality proved a horrifying burden.

CHAPTER 3

The moon had journeyed west across the night sky and was inching towards the mountain peaks in the distance. The rotting neighborhood was eerily quiet, as the wind had died to a hush. Grass swayed, insects chirped, and the mushy sounds of butchery lifted from the lonely intersection.

A large black pool had formed in the center and crept towards the curbs, reflecting a perfect moon on its glassy surface. Within it, a pair of severed arms rested in the muck, along with two legs, several organs, and multiple piles of carved flesh.

The maiden continued her work.

She hovered over the grisly remains of the brute, now reduced to an upper torso with a neck and head. Her cloak rested on the curb nearby, neatly folded beside an old dish towel. She wore a colorful apron with a cheerful kiss request, adding some unintended levity to the operation. The cleaver and carving knife came from the same withered kitchen. The former resident must have fancied themself a chef.

The brute was facedown in his own filth. He had passed out after screaming for the better part of an hour. It was a welcome peace that allowed the maiden to finish at her own pace. She threaded straps of polyester through the back of his ribcage, now exposed due to the removal of his trap muscles. A double weave around the bones pro-vided the sturdiness she needed, as it was a long journey to Denver and comfort would be paramount.

After a final loop around the neck, she clicked the buckle locks and cinched them tight. A definite shriek had the brute been conscious. The maiden climbed to her feet and rolled the aches from her shoul-ders. She raised her arms into a needed stretch and released a grunt of conclusion. Her eyes caught the setting moon, prompting a quick cal-culation. The resulting grimace pursed her cheeks, as she would not get far that night.

Alas, another day in Durango.

But without the scourge of hunters.

The maiden reached down, gripped the straps, and lifted the brute from the muck. His limp head dangled from the torso, adding a lop-sided weight to the pack. Not that she minded, as the proper carry would be quite different. His sodden chest and beard dripped blood as she walked over to the curb. She tossed him into the grass like a fleshy duffle bag, then nabbed the towel to wipe herself clean. A moderate wait would also do the job, as blood vanished into ash just like flesh and bone. But the rancid smell pestered her composure, and with moonlight wasting, better to clean up and hit the road with faculties intact.

The brute was still unconscious, but signs of healing were already apparent. The bleeding had stopped and wounds were beginning to scab. With enough time and proper care, even this level of mutilation could regenerate. But given the mental strain and lack of locomotion, most victims perished to the rising sun.

The maiden tossed the bloodied towel aside, then plucked her cloak from the curb. She slipped her arms inside and popped it over her shoulders. Motes of ash rose from the black pool and floated away, catching her eye. Random specks sparkled and faded like grisly fireflies. With a heavy sigh, the maiden snatched the straps and lifted the brute from the grass. She tossed him over her shoulder like a backpack. The weight of his limp head fell forward, pressing his chin to his chest. The moonlit speckles were increasing, beautiful in their finality, but the maiden could not enjoy them. She smiled at the sight, then turned away and walked towards the cul-de-sac.

A short minute later, she arrived back at the scene. A speckled cloud had formed where the slender man fell. It swirled inside the concrete circle like a lonely apparition. The other woman was still intact, lying facedown on the pavement. Not dead, but badly injured. Her brittle hands continued to claw at the cracked asphalt. Slowly, blindly, seeking shelter, but too weak to pull her body forward. The sun would finish her off, but the maiden was a greedy killer. She walked over, unsheathed her machete, and drove it through the woman's neck.

The hands went limp.

Blood pooled from the stump.

The maiden, having revealed her prize, knelt down to rip it from the flesh. She steadied the severed head with a foot, then reached into the cavity and closed her fist around the hyoid bone. A sharp yank tore it free. She rose to her feet with the bone in her grasp, cleansing the town of its filthy intrusion. The survivors would never know. They would continue to fear the hunters. They would continue to fear the maiden. But in that moment, none of it mattered. The deed was done, and the blood dripping from her fist was the only triumph she needed.

That is, until the next town.

The maiden resumed her trek.

* * *

An hour later, the moon kissed the mountain peaks and a dull orange glow appeared to the east. The maiden, mere minutes from the release of true death, walked casually through the main corridor of downtown Durango.

She feared nothing, for her destination approached.

The remains of abandoned shops flanked her to either side. Rusted cars lined the strip, now decades past their expired meters. Broken glass and debris littered the sidewalks. Nature had reclaimed the town, gifting shelter to its countless creatures. Birds nested on the shelves of old kitchens. Rats roamed freely between the walls. The boxy caves offered a reprieve to all, be it from the dead of night or peak of day.

The maiden glanced up to find her own haven, a local bank. She stepped onto the sidewalk and through the main doors, the panes of which rested on the pavement. Glass crunched beneath her feet as she strolled into the main lobby. The darkness welcomed her, as it always did. She hopped over a teller counter and landed on the other side. The impact forced a grunt from her companion, who was slowly emerging from shock. She paid him no mind as she ducked into a hallway and proceeded to the rear. Step by step, a silvery shelter revealed itself.

The vault.

Decades after the Great Onslaught, a depressing consistency plagued the bank vaults. They were always open, always plundered, and always lined with cots. In the first several years, vaults were seen as power grabs. Paper money had lost its value, but the allure of instant wealth was alive and well. As the years turned to decades, it wasn't uncommon to find sacks of cash out in the wild. The bags themselves contained more value, so finders would often dump the paper to collect a better resource. When a banknote floated in the wind, it served as a grim reminder. The pitfalls of greed extended beyond the pale.

Global anarchy turned the vaults into bunkers. Survivors claimed them as strongholds, which in turn attracted the hunters. The resulting slaughters stripped the vaults of appeal. As survivors fled into the mountains, the banks fell into disuse. They carried burdens of fear, like haunted houses nestled in the forest. Survivors chose the peaks. Hunters chose the sewers. The maiden, lurking comfortably in between, chose the solace of a stalemate.

The vault door was already cracked when she arrived. Its rectangular pane was several inches thick and tarnished from exposure. A far cry from the round behemoths in bigger cities, but more than enough to secure the funds of a smaller town. A firm tug opened the door, which whined upon its massive hinges. She glanced down the hallway as the first rays of sunlight punched through the exterior windows. Fingers of death, but well out of reach. She stepped inside the vault and closed the door behind her.

The door did not latch, as the mechanism was destroyed long ago. A long metal rod leaned against the wall inside, serving as a makeshift lock. Scratches in the door revealed the optimal angle, as employed by previous occupants. She pressed the rod to the wall and followed the marks. It slipped through the handles and locked into a crude catch on the other side. Hardly the most secure contraption, but also not important. The darkness enveloped her like a warm blanket. A true void, the life-giving serenity of regeneration.

But not just yet.

She retrieved a small flashlight from her satchel and gave it several shakes. Batteries were hard to come by, so kinetic chargers were much preferred. She clicked it on and panned a dim beam around the vault, revealing the usual cots and broken deposit boxes. A handful of banknotes were scattered across the floor, along with discarded keys and some worthless heirlooms. The usual funk of staleness teased her nostrils. She selected the cleanest cot, then dropped her unwelcome passenger onto the dirty concrete. His head and torso thumped the floor, expelling another grunt from his damaged lungs. The maiden stepped over to the cot and lowered herself onto the fabric. The rickety frame creaked and settled under the weight. Her shoulders slumped as the evening tension drained from her body.

The relief was bittersweet.

It was always bittersweet.

For the maiden stalks the night.

She unburdened herself and laid her trappings aside. The machete blade, now cleansed of its crimson sheen, clanked upon the floor. A weathered satchel thumped beside it. Her wearied flesh collapsed onto the cot, for the gift of restoration was imminent. As her mind drifted, she glanced at her mutilated companion. The meat squirmed like a sickly larva, struggling to emerge from its cocoon. The maiden sighed, then killed the flashlight and returned to the void.

* * *

Moan. Scratch. Moan. Scratch. Moan. Scratch.

The maiden opened her eyes, not that it helped. A cold and relentless darkness consumed her gaze. The ceiling above was meters away, perhaps miles. A strange noise had coaxed her out of a deep slumber, and it continued.

Moan. Scratch.

It would appear her consciousness was shared by another.

Her foggy mind pleaded to ignore the pest and reclaim the void. Her aching muscles, on the other hand, pleaded for a convenient snack. A rat, usually. Sometimes a possum or raccoon. But none were realistic, given the nature of her presence. This particular nuisance was self-inflicted. She quietly sighed, then closed the eyes that gave her no advantage.

"The beast awakens," she said softly.

"Wha ... where am I?" the brute said, his tone weak and garbled.

"Does it matter?"

"Did you ... take my eyes too?"

"Not yet."

"This ... this cruelty ... is beyond measure."

"You say that as if I suffer guilt."

A weighted pause infected the space. The brute fell into contemplation, assessing the dire situation as best he could. His head twisted back and forth, sending faint scratches into the air as his scraggly beard swept across the floor. The maiden remained silent, content to let her captive torture his own mind.

"Are you ... going to kill me?" the brute said.

"Clearly not my intent," the maiden said.

"But if you don't ... *they* will."

"Then it would seem your survival rests with me."

"A traitor."

"Only to the treacherous."

The brute grunted. "Keep ... keep reciting that fiction. Your death ... will be celebrated. Your terror ... will be but a memory."

"Is that envy I detect?"

Another weighted pause, this time without a squirm. The brute could sense the walls closing around him. The trap was set, and it's always better to stand behind the spring.

"I will tell you ... what you wish to hear."

"That much was assumed."

"Under one condition."

The maiden chuckled. "You mistake this for a negotiation."

"Not a bargain. Just ... just a promise."

"Speak your peace, then."

"If I'm to be a rat, then ... protect me from the serpents. I would rather ... greet the grave ... than return to their grasp."

"Your death, shall it come, will be mine and mine alone. That I can promise."

The brute groaned at the unsavory compromise. "Hand of the Bone Maiden. Not ... a life I had envisioned."

"None of this is life. That ended a long time ago."

Silence returned to the vault. The moaning stopped. The scratching stopped. A reluctant peace enveloped the space. Soon after, the void returned to swallow them both.

CHAPTER 4

Stab. Burn. Stab. Burn. Stab. Burn.

A steady and persistent pain pulled the brute from a heavy stupor. His head was bobbing and swaying to an unseen puppeteer, exacerbating the strain around his shoulders. He lifted his head, which immediately lessened the discomfort. The flesh around his upper ribs was still healing, but the interwoven straps had rubbed it raw. His lower ribs bore most of the weight, allowing fresh muscle to grow around the straps. The fusion offered a meager reprieve. As long as he stayed alert, he could manage the pain.

The roadway below him slowly trailed away. He followed the cracked pavement into the distance, where nothing of consequence caught his eye. Trees and mountains formed a charcoal skyline beneath the ever-present moonlight. Frogs and insects competed for attention. A sharp bouquet of pine teased his nose from every direction. His gaze lifted into the sky, where a faint glow to the west slowly departed.

The night was young.

And the world it cloaked was forever changed.

The gentle pats of footsteps found his ears, which perfectly mirrored his shifting flesh. The maiden had begun her long trek to Denver, and he was an unwilling passenger. He thought back to the cul-de-sac, where fear had finally caught up to him. Three trained hunters, scourge of the shadows, erased by the ultimate retribution.

The terror had turned against him.

And perhaps he should be grateful.

"Ten days," he said.

The maiden did not respond.

"If you plan to walk, you're looking at a ten-day journey to Denver. That's minimum if you don't stop. Sala may be gone by then."

The maiden kept walking.

"Wanna double back for a bike? Hell, I'd take a skateboard. Anything's faster than this shit."

The maiden kept walking.

The brute sighed. "So what's your name?"

No response.

"If I'm going to be your luggage, we might as well get to know each other. I'm Orin, by the way. I'm actually from Denver, so you picked the right handbag. Originally, I mean, before the war. Born and raised. Single mother, younger sister, deadbeat dad out of the picture. I also lived in Utah for a time. Moved there for a girl, but it didn't work out. Dumb mistake, but at least the sex was good."

"Quiet," the maiden said.

"Too graphic? I can tone it down if you w—" Orin fell from her grasp and slammed onto the pavement, bashing his head and knocking the wind from his chest. As he gasped for breath, his blurred vision caught a shadow vanishing into the woods.

The maiden had abandoned him.

His head began to throb, adding insult to a massive array of injuries. He glanced left to a bank of trees, then right to a bank of trees, then pinched his eyes shut and pressed his forehead to the pavement. "So that's it then," he said with a pained sigh. "Hi, I'm Orin. I'm a Scorpio. I like scuba diving and long walks on the beach. Dumbass." He continued to grouse as the countdown to true death ticked inside his head. His grumbles grew weaker, and weaker, then stopped. The forest reclaimed his ears, and the loneliness it brought was deafening.

Moments later, a heavy thump on the pavement rattled his torso.

He yelped with fright and whipped his gaze to the source, uncovering a wall of brown fur. Further inspection revealed the carcass of a freshly killed deer.

And then, without warning, he was in the air again.

He glided over the corpse like a gory marionette. After a brief flight, the maiden dropped him facedown onto the creature's neck. The flesh was still warm. A deathly odor flooded his nostrils and goaded his predator instincts. But he hesitated. Fear had overtaken desire. And so he waited, petrified to continue living.

The maiden knelt down into his peripheral view. Blood soaked her face from chin to nose. Orin could smell the life-giving nectar. The richness of the iron. The sweetness of the protein. The veins beneath his quivering chin were brimming with it.

"Eat," she said.

And so he did, grateful for every second.

* * *

The pair had traveled into the morning hours and climbed higher into the Rockies. The cold was threatening at that point, so care would be needed for the daylight hours. They straddled the invisible line between immortals and survivors. It was the best place to traverse, as neither side wanted to risk ambush by the other. But even so, vigilance guided safe passage.

Orin had learned to counter sway, making the jaunt less painful. The occasional grunt broke the silence as the maiden shifted her burden. The roadway continued to pass beneath them. Orin picked random trees and watched them slowly fade into the distance. Partly to distract himself, and partly to gauge progress. They were making good time, as best he could tell.

The maiden would halt every now and then to suss out a disturbance. Her tracking prowess had reached considerable heights through the years. She could identify species and quantity on sound alone. "Four elk," she might say under her breath before resuming the trek. An impressive talent, even to a seasoned hunter.

As the hours passed, the moon began its slow descent towards the horizon. Orin kept a close eye, assuming the role of timekeeper. He awaited the moment of contact, which permitted some vocal dignity. "Moon's getting really low," he said.

No response.

Orin waited a few seconds, then sighed. "Not to question your judgment, but I'd be looking for a place to—"

The maiden ducked forward to examine the pavement, jostling the weight on her back. Orin yelped with pain and grumbled some curses. Not loud enough to attract attention, but more than enough to register the complaint.

"Easy on the meat, lass," he said.

No response.

Orin remained awkwardly suspended for a time as the maiden studied a series of markings etched into the concrete. The symbols were familiar to her eyes, human glyphs used to transfer intel between camps. Similar to hieroglyphs, their placement and quantity denoted phrases and concepts. They read, *haven half-mile right rabbit.*

"There's a safehouse ahead. We'll stay there tonight."

Orin lifted an eyebrow. "Um, not to point out the obvious—"

"It's fine. Nobody's home."

"How do you know?"

"The markings are three variants behind. Whoever left them is long gone."

"Or dead."

"Or dead," the maiden said, then resumed her trek down the roadway.

Half a mile later, her eyes were fixed to the forest line on the right-hand side. Her sharpened gaze scanned for the telltale symbol. Before long, she locked onto the oval knot of a large aspen tree. A pair of prominent grooves sloped off to one side, like the ears of a rabbit. She stepped off the pavement and approached the tree, behind which was the start of a well-hidden nature path. The moon had begun its slow dive behind the mountains, as if to secure its own hideaway. The maiden gave it a final glance, then vanished into the forest.

The trail dipped into a large gully after several minutes, revealing an old stone cabin built inside it. The water channel had been diverted, leaving it to settle without risk of flooding. A thick canopy of aspen and fir trees kept it out of sight. The air was noticeably colder, thanks to longer hours bathed in shadow. A concern, but not a deterrent. Vines and weeds had overtaken the exterior, giving it a distinct European flair. But with time a luxury, the structural admiration would have to wait.

She approached the front entry with little caution, as no signs of recent use were apparent. The door was still attached, but the latch had been ripped from the pane. Perhaps a kick, maybe a hasty exit. In any case, the last occupants were met with an unseen violence. The maiden pressed her hand to the pane and gave it a gentle push.

The door whined open, revealing the dark confines of a long-neglected haven. She fished the flashlight from her satchel and clicked it on. Bats detached from the ceiling and fled through an open window. The maiden did not flinch. She panned the beam around the interior, uncovering soiled furniture, dusty shelves, and a wood-burning stove with logs still inside. Despite the filthy furnishings, the structure was remarkably sound. The cone of light continued around the space and settled on a floor hatch in the rear. The maiden stepped over, gripped the handle, and yanked it open. She shined the light into an old cellar, no doubt used as a last resort should hunters comb the area. "That'll do," she said, then flipped the hatch shut.

She removed Orin from her back and placed him in a ratty chair next to the stove, taking time to prop him up for comfort. He shifted against the armrest while the maiden turned her attention to the stove. After a quick inspection, she retrieved a matchbox from her satchel and lit the logs, using some old cloth as kindling. The flames quickly took hold and the cabin filled with a muted glow. The maiden removed her blade and satchel, then dropped them beside a shabby couch. It faced the chair with a small table in between, creating a rustic living space. She took a moment to close the window, then parked her tired body on the dusty cushions.

A grim silence infected the cabin. The pops of burning wood

needled a growing tension. Orin stared at the maiden while she stared at the glowing stove. Her mind was distant. It wrestled with an unknown entity, unconcerned with the plights of the physical realm. Orin, never one to let a sleeping dog lie, decided to break the ice.

"This reminds me of camping," he said with a slight grin.

The maiden did not respond.

Orin grimaced, then shifted his gaze to the flames. "I used to love camping. Sitting around the fire, cooking hotdogs and cutting up. Ah, good times. Funny story, I was actually out in the wild when the war started. I was drinking coffee in a tent near Vail as the Great Onslaught raged out of sight. I emerged from the wilderness into total devastation. Chaos, slaughter, like being ported to a fucked-up Narnia. I was days late to the party, so to speak. Got turned a week later." He huffed and shook his head. "I should have stayed in the woods." His eyes shifted back to the maiden. "What about you? Remember where you were when the world ended?"

"I remember the exact moment," the maiden said. "I was living in Durham, North Carolina when the Onslaught hit. College town, lots of young folk and evening turnover, good hub for vamps. I had met up with some friends at a local bar. Dain's Place on 9th. We were drinking beers and enjoying some pub grub. I had ordered wings and fries."

Orin snorted. "A vamp eating chicken?"

"I know." She rolled her eyes and smirked at Orin, as if slightly embarrassed. "I like Buffalo sauce, what can I say?"

Orin grinned.

"My friends were all human, so it was to fit in more than anything. They were all professor types, the kind that like to drink fancy brews while debating current events. I enjoyed the banter, even though I had lived through much of the precedent they cited. I like strong flavors, and the sauce at Dain's was to die for. It was a good time. A calm and peaceful time. Which made the breaking news that much more devastating."

Her gaze returned to the crackling fire. "I will never forget that moment. Every television got interrupted by the national broadcast system. That godawful tone. Cut through the room like a knife through butter. The reporter was nervous, flustered, needed to gather himself. He took a deep breath, then said, 'It is of paramount importance that you pay close attention to what I am about to say. It will be hard to digest and tempting to dismiss. But I assure you, with God as my witness, every detail is real.' I knew at that moment. That horrible, horrible moment. Human rule over the planet had come to an end."

"One might argue the opposite," Orin said. "In that *glorious* moment, the true masters of Earth rose up to claim their rightful throne."

The maiden met eyes with Orin. Her cold and clinical gaze was hard to read, as if staring into the deadness of a plastic doll. "You're not wrong," she said with a flat tone. "Nations rise and fall all the time. Cultures clash, ideas get reinvented. And in the darkness, we always survive." Her gaze floated back to the fire. "But there is a very big difference between conquest and extermination. I have watched the madmen of history try to birth their utopias. They always fail, and their visions are always condemned by history."

She returned her gaze to Orin, this time with a hardened expression. "When the dust finally settles, and the immortal wake reveals its righteous civilization, how do you think history will regard its genocidal birth?"

Orin thought for a moment before responding. "So that's why you do it," he said through contemplation. "You're trying to save our souls."

"In a way," she said, then released a heavy sigh. "I just want the bullies of this world to fear something greater than loss of power."

Orin paused again, this time to shrink inside his own head. The past enveloped him, and for the first time since it all began, he sensed a repercussion. His mutilation was more backlash than burden. His tone softened as he peered beyond the maiden. "Bullies like Sala Rain."

She nodded. "Sala and his raiders terrorized the Gulf Coast for years. I cannot begin to quantify his ruin. Remember that little girl and the rapist?" The maiden sighed and pursed her lips. "I tracked him from the Panhandle to Mexico, picking off raiders and sub-units along the way. And then, *poof.* He disappeared without a trace."

"To create the Rainmaker Faction."

"Yup. Years later, he emerged from the abyss with even more power. I finally got a bead on his posse in El Paso. Been tracking him ever since. The route went cold after a time, never knew why. I interrogated as best I could, but intel was depressingly thin. It was like he dropped off the planet. But then," she said with a hint of mockery, "I tagged a hunter who shed some light on the mystery. Apparently, Sala fucked-off to Denver to partner with warlord Malin."

Orin grinned.

The maiden softened her expression, inviting him to speak his mind.

"The Rainmakers were absorbed into the Malin Cartel," Orin said. "They still exist, but now serve as a recruitment sect. Some still hunt. Most stick to the network."

"Are you a Rainmaker?"

"No," Orin said hastily. "But I've encountered many. I'm part of a peripheral unit. Small-time, nameless. Same deal, though. Got absorbed and now work as hunters." He glanced away and sighed. "It's the only game in town these days."

"You mentioned a coming union. What is that about?"

"Like you said, the NWS controls everything west of the Mississippi. As I understand it, that border is about to become obsolete."

"They're expanding coast to coast?"

"No. Continent to continent."

The maiden flinched. It was subtle, but enough to catch the eye of an experienced hunter. The ghost, it would seem, had become corporeal.

"That's all I know," Orin said, hoping to end his part.

The maiden retreated into her mind, offering no resolution.

Orin seized the moment. "This is not a gang of disorganized thugs. You're dealing with real power now. Tangible influence on a global scale. Sala is in the belly of that beast. Perhaps this isn't a mark that can be erased."

A brief silence infected the space.

The maiden nodded slowly as she weighed the situation. Embers popped in the background, cutting through the stillness like beating drums. She took a deep breath, then emptied her lungs and snapped back to a steely persona. "We should get some rest."

Orin closed his eyes and screamed inside his head.

The maiden rose to her feet and walked over to the stove. She latched the door shut and secured the spark screen, ensuring that their slumber would not end in flames. The crackling embers continued to battle the evening chill. They would die in the morning hours and pass their duty to the sun, protecting the tenants until the next evening. The maiden turned her attention to Orin. She grabbed the straps and pulled him into the air, this time with enough care to spare him discomfort. He did not grouse or whimper, which the maiden mistook for gratitude. His despair endured as she carried him down into the cellar.

CHAPTER 5

Orin awoke to excruciating pain. His eyelids snapped open, revealing beams of broken light dancing around him. He was facedown on a filthy stone floor. Still in the cellar, but away from the tattered sack on which he fell asleep. The base of a ladder stood beside him. The scattered light merged into a single cone, at which point he recognized the source.

A flashlight.

And then the smell of blood.

And then the pain erased it all.

Burning, piercing, stabbing pain. His back was on fire, yet there was no smoke to blame. No water to ease the suffering. He could only writhe and wail as the agony consumed him.

"Shut up," the maiden said from above. She was tending to the injury, albeit not in the gentlest of manners.

"What the—*aah*—fuck happened?"

"You caught a rusty nail as I was carrying you up. Gashed your back. Now shut the fuck up while I close the wound."

"Since when—*ergh*—do you care about—*ugh*—closing my wounds?"

"Since you became my guide. The quicker you heal, the less you whine."

"*Ergh*—fuck you, too."

The maiden chuckled softly, which ended with a sharp rip.

Orin turned his head. "Is that duct tape?"

"Feel free to pass the gauze and saline if you prefer."

Orin closed his eyes and plunked his head on the floor.

"Here." She grabbed the handle of an old tool and stuffed it into his mouth. "Bite down and don't scream. Shouldn't take but a moment."

Orin's eyes watered as the pain shot from bad to worse. The maiden pressed the wound together with her hand and knee, then bound it with tape. She proceeded down the gash until every inch was covered. Orin buried his teeth into the wooden handle as tears dripped from his pinched eyelids. He groaned and trembled, but did not scream. The maiden secured the bandage with a few more strips, then returned the tape roll to her satchel. She plopped onto the floor next to Orin and released a heavy sigh.

"Good job," she said, then patted his sweating scalp.

Orin spat out the handle and fought to slow his breathing. His eyes remained shut as he willed the pain back to a reasonable level. "Thanks," he said between labored breaths.

"Welcome." Blood dripped from her hands and plinked the floor, adding a grim melody to the cellar. "You also broke a rib, by the way. Should feel a nagging sting for a while."

"Huh? How did that happen?"

"Lost my balance on the ladder. Had to drop you."

Orin huffed. "I retract my thanks."

The maiden snickered. "You'll heal up soon enough."

Orin opened his eyes and turned to meet the maiden's gaze. "So what now?"

She sighed and glanced around the filthy cellar. It radiated surrender, from cobwebs to rotten shelves. Roots from nearby trees poked through cracks in the walls. Just a hole in the world that time forgot. It had served its purpose and returned to the insects.

Her eyes wandered back to Orin. "Want some breakfast?"

* * *

An hour later, the trek to Denver had resumed. The maiden cruised down the roadway with Orin on her back. The ride had decreased in comfort, thanks to the fresh wound on his back. He coped as best he could, leaning into every step to dull the pain. The broken rib jabbed his flesh with each sway, which somewhat negated the benefit. Desperate for a distraction, he pondered something to talk about. And then his tongue provided a topic. Having found another strand of wool, he spit it out with some extra drama and decided to offer commentary.

"It's an unpopular opinion," he said, "but I really like sheep blood. Not the wild Big Horns, but those old farm breeds. It's easy on the stomach, not that I have the pleasure of a stomach at the moment. I should speak to management about that."

The maiden snickered.

"What about you? Got a favorite red?"

"Bordeaux."

"Holy shit," Orin said with a mocking laugh. "She has a sense of humor, ladies and gentlemen. I would really like to slow clap at the moment."

The maiden slowly clapped.

"Thank you," Orin said. "You're a very kind sadist."

"I think camel is my favorite."

"*Camel?* Where the hell did you find camel?"

"Morocco. Spent several decades there. They're not as abundant as they once were, back when I called it home."

"When was that?"

"About 600 years ago."

The statement caught Orin off-guard. He started to respond, but stammered instead. The number rattled inside his head, like a fork in a garbage disposal. He peered over his shoulder and dropped the jokey tone. "How old are you?"

"That's not a polite thing to ask."

"Apologies. But you can't drop a number like that and not expect a follow-up question."

The maiden did not respond.

Silence settled between them, and for once, Orin allowed it to rest. He chewed on his lip as a reminder not to speak. His mind, on the other hand, had found its distraction.

* * *

The maiden crested a steep hill that overlooked a mountain valley. A fog bank had rolled in and settled atop the canopy, like a fluffy blanket pulled across the treetops. Several tips were still visible under the moonlight, along with a handful of buildings and a water tower. A small town rested beneath the fog, shielding its sprawl from prying eyes. The maiden paused to gather what little info she could. Orin continued to fret inside his own head. His gaze remained locked to the pavement behind them as his mind ventured elsewhere.

The maiden stared at the water tower. Its bulbous top floated just above the fog, like a boat lost in open waters. Its anchor-like stilts punched through the haze and down to the ground. The letters that proudly proclaimed its locale were too dim to read. But at that moment, sight was not the most intriguing sense. The ceaseless drone of insects had gained an additional voice.

Many voices, it would seem.

The distant roar of conversation.

It was brazened and open, like a community gathering. Its beneficiaries had no concern for secrecy. Definitely not human, lest they carry a death wish. Drunken vamps, perhaps. An odd sense of disrespect teased the maiden's conscience. Clearly her work was underappreciated. But then the paranoia seeped in. Perhaps her reputation had created a monster, a true threat, and she was walking into a trap. In either case, a stealthy approach was critical.

"Town ahead," she said softly.

"Why are you whispering?" Orin said, matching her pitch.

"Because it's inhabited."

"Us or them?"

"Don't know. Can't tell yet."

"*Yet.* So you're going in."

"It's what I do."

"Why risk it? Just avoid the hassle and walk around."

"The shark goes where it wants. It doesn't fear the minnows."

"You're not a fucking fish, lady," Orin said a little louder.

"Shh."

Orin sighed.

The maiden scanned the area as best she could. A cluster of treetops poked above the fog near the main strip. "We'll approach from the grove."

"Like I have a say. There's no *we* in this shanty."

"Shush."

Orin grimaced as the maiden resumed her trek. She glided down the roadway towards the hidden valley, using the soft steps of a mounting ambush. As she dipped beneath the fog, her path veered into the forest. She floated through the trees like a stalking panther. Every breath a hush. Every step a careful calculation. The voices grew louder as she neared the town perimeter. Numerous voices, too many to count. Definitely not the howls of drunkards. There was purpose in the air, a drumming of events to come.

She pushed through the grove and settled at the tree line, using a large oak as cover. A small park separated her from a row of abandoned buildings along the main strip, the rear facades of a bygone era. She peered around the trunk and panned across the field. No watchers, no hunters, just a rusted swing set creaking in the breeze. She emerged from the forest and darted through the grass, taking refuge inside an old loading bay.

She melded into the shadows and paused to listen, verifying that her approach had gone unseen. The filthy interior had succumbed to the elements. It stank of damp moss and rotten wood. Pastel walls and dusty vases revealed the workspace of an old flower shop. The maiden stepped towards the front, choosing her path carefully. As she neared the main window, a strange light began to emerge. Dim at first, but then a distinct pair. She settled beneath the sill and wiped away some grime to uncover the source.

A transport truck.

It idled in the street with multiple vampires clamoring around it.

Her gaze shifted to the rear, where another pair of headlights glowed behind it. Then another, and another. An entire caravan with dozens of vampires barking orders.

Hunters in rugged hide.

Sentries in tactical gear.

An operation was afoot.

"Ninety percent capacity," someone said. "One more stop then back."

"ETA 0300," another said.

The maiden watched as a hunter chatted with a sentry, then stepped around a truck and climbed inside. The conversation was muffled, but the body language told her everything she needed to know.

"It's an evac," she said softly. "They're recalling the hunters."

"An *evac*? What the hell for?"

"Beats me. But I intend to find out."

"How? Gonna stroll up and ask?"

"Yeah."

"That was a joke. I was joking."

"No one knows me. We'll just play the part."

"I *am* the part, if you recall. It may be more than a little suspicious to mosey up with a butchered hunter on your back."

"Trust me."

The maiden doubled back through the flower shop and exited through the loading bay. She hurried past several buildings, opting to meet the caravan head-on. After a brief amble down an alley, she emerged onto the main roadway. The headlights shined a block away, but not enough to reveal her presence.

Yet.

"Follow my lead," she said, then started jogging towards the lead truck.

Orin opted not to respond, as the sudden bouncing jabbed his flesh. He gnashed his teeth and grunted with discomfort as the maiden approached.

Moments later, the veil was lifted. "Yo!" the maiden shouted with arms overhead, making sure to grab a sentry's attention before slowing her jog. A stout woman in tactical gear turned to meet her arrival. The maiden slowed to a stroll and started panting, as if to conclude a long run. "Holy hell," she said between labored breaths. "Thought I wouldn't make it." She gripped her waist and took her final steps.

"Who are you?" the sentry said.

"The Bone Maiden. Obviously."

The sentry grunted into a grin. "Cute."

"Sloan West, unaffiliated."

"Unaffiliated?"

"Former 505."

The sentry grimaced. "Ugh, sorry."

"Meh. Win some, lose some. Oh, speaking of which—" She whipped around to reveal Orin, who released another pained grunt. "Found one of your idiots in Durango."

The woman gasped and took a step back. "Fuck me."

"No," Orin said. "Definitely fuck *me.*"

"What the hell happened to you?"

"Goddamn bear, of all things. Killed my partner and nearly killed me, if not for *this* lovely dose of ex machina." He nodded back to the maiden. "Gonna hit the ward back in Denver, see what they can do."

"You're in luck," the sentry said with a more affable tone. "That's where we're headed. One more stop, then back to basecamp."

"Hear that?" the maiden said. "Finally caught a break."

"About damn time." Orin moaned with contentment, then grinned at the sentry. "I really want to hug you right now."

"Pass," the woman said, but appreciated the humor.

"So what the hell is going on here? I didn't expect to see transporters this far in."

"Total recall. All hunters are to report back to headquarters. Malin is addressing the cartel in a couple days. He wants everyone present."

"Why?"

"Some big announcement."

"About the union?" the maiden said with interest.

"Maybe. Not for me to know."

"So what do we do?" Orin said. "Just hop on a truck?"

"In due time." She eyed the maiden. "Please hold out your hand."

The maiden raised an eyebrow. "Why?"

"No hand, no truck. Your choice."

She hesitated, but then lifted a hand off to the side.

The sentry plucked a small flashlight from her utility belt, making sure to point it downward. She uncapped the bulb and clicked it on, painting a small purple dot on the ground. "Stand still," she said. "You don't want this in your eyes."

The maiden gulped.

The sentry lifted the UV light and shined it on the maiden's hand. The pain was instant, like touching a hot stove. Instinct yanked her flesh away and waved it in the chilled air. A thin line of smoke departed the skin, now red and blistered.

She growled in discomfort. "What the fuck?"

"Sorry," the sentry said. "This is human territory. Can't be too careful."

"Could've just asked."

"Protocol." The woman shrugged, then pointed towards the rear trucks. "Back one is empty, just hop in there. We'll be on our way in a minute."

The maiden sneered, then proceeded down the line.

"No check for me?" Orin said as they walked away. "That hurts my feelings."

The sentry snickered, then went about her business.

*   *   *

The trucks were old military transports, troop carriers with lots of armor and little comfort. They rarely left the highways, as human sabotage was a common tactic. They also consumed a ton of precious fuel, so their usage was limited to critical projects. Faction leaders used them to travel between bases. But otherwise, they rarely left the strongholds.

Orin and the maiden bounced around the rear cargo hold. The benches were made of cold metal, not ideal for sore bodies. The maiden had propped Orin to her side and draped an arm across his chest, giving him a much-needed reprieve. But as the caravan began its journey, it quickly became the worst option. Thus, the maiden hoisted him into her lap and clutched him like a pillow. It afforded them some travel peace, as anyone boarding the truck had zero interest to learn more about them.

The ride was swift and efficient, as lingering around the mountains was a risky endeavor. Sentries kept watchful eyes on the periphery, but as the landscape flattened, so did passenger nerves. Before long, a calmness had enveloped the cabin. A sense of safety washed over the group, allowing the collective tension to abate.

Save for one.

The maiden stirred inside her head.

An hour into the trip, she spotted something peculiar. The Denver skyline revealed itself through the rear gate. Black towers raised into the sky, cutting through a sheet of stars. But the image was moving away. She realized that the caravan had traveled around the perimeter and was now headed east.

"Where are we going?" she whispered to Orin.

"Denver," he whispered back. "Thought that was obvious."

"But I can see the city. We're heading in the wrong direction."

"Not *that* Denver."

CHAPTER 6

The caravan rumbled around a sharp corner, forcing everyone inside to counter lean. The maiden palmed the wall for support, which gave her a clear view of the rear gate. A rusty green sign snapped into view and began its long fade into the distance. A white airplane was stamped on its face, denoting a throughway to the Denver Airport. The mystery deepened, as she hadn't heard the roar of a jet engine for the better part of a century.

A few minutes later, the caravan rolled into the departures lane and slowed to a stop. The corridor was well-lit, much to her surprise. A crowd had gathered and was disarmingly calm, as if waiting to attend a lecture. Hunters in rugged hides mingled with brokers in three-piece suits. Gowns, ties, and other high fashion flowed freely around the space. There were even cocktails in the grips of manicured hands, a sight that seemed unusually distant. The truck had transformed into a rabbit hole, and the maiden was peering through the looking glass.

A sentry in tactical gear stepped around to the rear gate. "Everyone out," she said, then unlatched and swung it open. The whine of old hinges was lost to the surrounding clamor. The passengers got up without much fuss and began to unload. "Cannot wait for a hot shower," one of them said before dropping to the pavement.

The maiden, having been first to board, was now last to depart. She continued to clutch Orin like a security blanket. Emerging from the awning, she stood tall on the rear ledge and panned her gaze across the gathering. The casual banter and lack of hostility infected her with a biting sense of displacement. Vampires talking, not tussling. Joking, mingling, shedding pretense like an old skin. Her jaw slacked and her mind recoiled, as if jolted from an 80-year dream.

"Let's go, sweetie," the sentry said.

"Oh, sorry," the maiden said, then dropped to the pavement.

The sentry stepped around the truck and slapped the side panel. "Loaded out," she yelled, prompting the drivers to depart. As the caravan crept away, a peculiar sound displaced the engines. The maiden stepped onto the curb and twisted in a slow circle, trying to locate the strange melody.

An *actual* melody.

Music.

With live instruments.

The enchantment was swift and complete. A smile stretched across her face as she walked towards the terminal entrance. The doors sensed her presence and slid open, giving her a nasty fright. She flinched backwards and into the person behind her. Hasty apologies poured from her mouth, which the well-dressed man politely dismissed. A minor accident, but grounds for battle in the unforgiving wilderness. And so she stood there, squeezing her blanket, utterly baffled by the truth she occupied.

"Welcome to Denver," Orin said, then turned to mutter over his shoulder. "Word to the wise, if you don't act normal, then people will see you as abnormal."

The maiden took a needed breath, then patted Orin's chest. "Noted."

"Just walk inside. Don't worry, you're among friends."

The maiden rolled her eyes, then proceeded into the terminal.

A vibrant collage of sound and color greeted her entrance. The entire space pulsed with activity. Ticket counters had transformed into makeshift bars. They served drinks to anyone willing, and most were.

Artistic murals danced across old monitors, adding a liveliness to the background. Décor was posh and abundant, from marble sculptures to gaudy chandeliers. An elevated platform housed a classical band clothed in black suits. They worked through a set of Mozart as if the Titanic had never sunk.

The maiden added a grunting chuckle to her disbelief.

"My stars," a woman said as she swiftly approached. A flowing gown trailed behind her as stiletto heels clacked upon the tile floor. The maiden tensed before she realized who the woman was addressing. "Orin! What happened to you?"

"Sandra," Orin said with a sudden stammer, but quickly regained his wits. "Long story involving a cuddly bear. Turns out they're quite dangerous."

The woman chuckled and sipped her martini, clearly undeterred by the severity. "You got a long stay in the ward ahead of you."

"That's the plan, but I need to speak with Sala first. He around?"

She gestured towards the gate checks. "Back in the sanctum as far as I know. I saw him yesterday, but we didn't chat. Malin has him quite busy at the moment."

"Thanks."

"Cheers." She met eyes with the maiden. "And who is this?"

"Ah yes. Sandra, Sloan. Sloan, Sandra."

"A pleasure," the maiden said.

"Mine as well."

"She's my knightess in shining armor," Orin said. "Saved me from that unfortunate cuddle. It's her first time in Denver, gonna show her around."

"Ah, welcome," Sandra said with an uptick. "Do not hesitate to seek me out, should you need anything. Clothes, food, the Rainmakers will provide."

Orin closed his eyes.

"Thank you," the maiden said. "That's very generous."

Sandra raised her glass for a solitary toast. "The best to both of you."

"Thanks," Orin said, then opened his eyes and smiled. "Gonna need it."

Sandra offered a subtle nod, then whisked away to her next repartee.

The maiden stood silently with her nails digging into Orin's flesh.

"I can explain," he said with a harsh whisper. "But first we need to get to Concourse C."

The maiden did not respond.

"If I wanted to rat you out, I would have already. I have as much to lose as you do."

The maiden closed her eyes and retreated to the void, the only place that welcomed her like an old friend. The nothingness enveloped her like a warm blanket. The discord departed, leaving her to the maw of an alternate universe. She was alone, unknown, a tumor inside the beast. And the time had come to spread. Her eyelids opened and the enemy reclaimed her, albeit without its knowledge. She softened her grip on Orin and stepped towards the gates.

Having spent eight decades stalking the wilderness, the chaos of a crowded terminal was a sensory assault. Bright lights and blinking neon pestered the maiden from every direction. The constant drone of background noise dulled her auditory sharpness. Evasion consumed most of her focus, as the last thing she needed was to draw any unwanted attention. The mangled torso in her grasp hooked enough curious glances to test her mettle.

Despite the relentless churn, distant memories bubbled from the depths. The smell of cigarettes, and the 50s era fashion that exhaled them. The freedom of post-war travel, and greeting friends at the gates when their red-eyes landed. The horrors of terrorism, and the newfound relegation to land and sea.

A dream, perhaps.

The chatter quieted as they neared a security check. No lines, no machines, just an unseen obligation to respect the rules. Sentries guarded the passage like bouncers at a nightclub. Their job was obvious to a fault: look for anyone who didn't belong.

"There's a protocol," Orin said. "Weapons aren't allowed inside the concourses. So when you reach the gate check, you need to drop them at holding. You'll be watched, so just act like you've done it before. Got it?"

The maiden grunted.

"I'll take that as a yes. Otherwise, we're both dead."

Several large tables enclosed a barricaded section. Behind them, numerous racks and bins housed weapons and luxury goods. A strange disconnect, as the expensive furs of high society floated above the tarnished blades of hunters. It would seem that comfort was paramount across the board, as no one wanted to lug unnecessary weight into social functions.

The maiden approached the table with an annoyed expression, trying to convey a waning patience. Just another gruesome delivery. The holding guard cared not in the slightest, as the sentient torso was enough to garner his full attention. Orin smiled just before he was abruptly dropped onto the table like a handbag. He barked on impact, but chose not to grouse. Some of the sentries would no doubt recognize him, so perhaps a pleasantry was in order.

"Hey guys," he said with a joking tone. "I'm waving with my brain."

The maiden unhooked her machete and snatched a dagger from her boot. She clanked them together and dropped them on the table. The checking guard, still entranced by the torso, slowly grabbed them and eyed the bins.

"Bin 12," he said.

"Gravy," the maiden said, then yanked Orin off the table.

"Hey," Orin said with a hint of bother. "Easy on the package, princess."

The maiden ignored him as she proceeded through the checkpoint. Several ports led into the concourse, each guarded by a sentry. She paused to adjust her satchel, allowing a brief study of etiquette as others passed. No gestures or decorum, just a simple saunter. She picked a lane and pushed forward, keeping her gaze locked onto the space beyond. But as she stepped into the port, the sentry palmed her shoulder.

The maiden flinched, enough to jostle Orin into a yelp. Instinct drove her hand to a machete handle that wasn't there. Her muscles tightened as adrenaline flooded her veins. First strike was out of the question, so she braced for a swift retaliation.

"The fuck, Orin?" the sentry said.

Orin scoffed. "I know, right? I'm a goddamn pool toy."

"What happened?"

"Long story. Many beers needed. Gotta debrief, then I'll fill you in."

"Alright. Best to ya," the sentry said, then eyed the maiden. "Sorry to startle you."

"No worries," she said, adding a smile.

The guard nodded. "Enjoy your evening."

They continued through the port and disappeared into the concourse. Their lungs emptied in a shared release of tension. No words needed, as the narrowness was fully understood.

The maiden paused inside a main junction. The gated wings of Concourse A stretched to either side. In front, the pedestrian bridge to Concourse B. Vamps of all persuasions flowed in every direction. Their interests bounced from gate to gate, group to group. Plush seating filled the waiting areas, long stripped of their torturous plastic benches. Wait staff floated around the bustle, serving drinks and morsels to the masses.

The maiden scanned each corridor, her anxious gaze hunting for amnesty. She spotted a family bathroom nearby, the old changing rooms for breeding mortals. A well-dressed couple emerged from within. They giggled and eyed each other with carnal intent, no doubt having blessed the space with their own lustful aromas. The maiden jumped at the opportunity and hurried over to the bathroom. She ducked inside, locked the door, then dropped Orin into the sink basin. His head thumped the mirror behind him, drawing a pained grunt.

"So you're one of them," she said. "You're a Rainmaker."

"Yes."

"You lied to me."

"I lied to stay alive." He groaned and shifted his back for comfort. "You of all people can sympathize with that, *Sloan*. Or whatever the fuck your name is. Like it or not, our wants are currently aligned."

She sneered, then snapped forward and clawed his neck. Her vise-like grip pressed his flesh against the mirror, staining it with his filth. "I should bleed you right here, leave you to die in a fucking airport toilet."

"Good luck getting to Sala without me," he said, wheezing.

Anger goaded her to open his throat, to seek her prize and vanish. But the path was set, the finish line was close, and there was no turning back. She released her grip and folded her arms, caging the beast within.

"I have a debt," Orin said between coughs. "My life isn't worth a regen. The second I enter Sala's lair, that's my death sentence. I only have one play left. I need you to kill Sala and then John Doe me at the ward." He coughed again and slumped back, weary and broken. "I can get you in, but I need you to get me out. That's the deal."

The maiden thought for a moment. "And why not do it myself?"

Orin chuckled. "Be my guest. I bet you don't make it to the bodyguards before the Makers cut you down."

"Bodyguards?"

"Two of them. Meathead types who shadow Sala wherever he goes. You'll have to deal with them too, but I can get you into the room. Until then, I'm your key."

"How?"

"There are two checkpoints, one at the gangway and one at the plane. Each requires a code unique to the Rainmakers."

"So tell me the code."

Orin huffed. "They don't know you, princess. You might as well tell them that you tortured a hunter for intel, which you technically did."

The maiden grimaced.

"At this very moment, you're nothing more than a flesh chauffeur. You have to drive me to the end to claim your bounty."

She sighed, then nodded.

"Speaking of which, I hope you're as good with your hands as you are with a blade."

"I can manage," she said, then lifted Orin from the basin.

CHAPTER 7

The maiden maintained a steady pace over the first pedestrian bridge. The tunnel was wide and pleasantly lit, serving as an artery between concourses. Traffic was constant, but less dense and chaotic. Floor-to-ceiling windows covered each wall, offering elevated views of the tarmac. Every gate was attached to a parked plane. Some retained their glossy sheens and engines, as if ready to depart. Others were dilapidated shells. But all were disabled and immobile. The lack of activity created a painting of an airport, a snapshot of what used to be. Sentries patrolled the grounds under the glare of spotlights, as security remained a principal concern. Many planes were lit from within. One emitted a kaleidoscope of colors, catching the maiden's gaze.

"What are those lights?" she said to Orin, still tight in her grasp.

Orin glanced at the tarmac. "It's a dance club."

"In a plane?"

"Yeah, why not?"

"Hmm, seems impractical."

"It's not like they're flying anywhere. Most were sabotaged during the war, but their bones are still good, so might as well use them. They've been converted to offices, lounges, brothels, whatever the public fancies."

"Where does everyone go when the sun comes up?"

"This is only the top of Denver, sweetheart. Think of it like the leisure level. There's an entire world beneath us, a huge network of hostels, day facilities, merchants, you name it. Malin spent the last decade creating an inverted city. It even has an underground transit that connects to the old downtown."

"Why not use the existing city?"

"We did, but the sprawl made it too easy for spies to infiltrate. The airport is disconnected from the city. Makes it easier to defend."

"Hmm," the maiden said with subtle reverence. "Smart play."

"That's Malin for you. Dude knows how to look ahead."

They passed through the junction for Concourse B and into the next pedestrian bridge. C42 was their destination, as instructed by Orin. The corridor was much less crowded, as Concourse C was reserved for leadership and admin staff. Most of the planes were superjumbos, the flying cities of aviation's peak. The maiden never had the pleasure, as most were constructed during the post-9/11 era. The planes seemed fictional in a way, monsters of immobility that looked as aerial as cargo ships.

The roar of congregation faded into the background as they emerged into the final junction. Suits and coffee mugs replaced gowns and martinis. Desks and file stores flanked the gates. The lighting was stark and sterile, almost hostile in its diffusion. A severity loomed over the space, as if to radiate its dominance over the world.

The maiden, cloaked in the rags of hardship, was rendered out of place. She hooked a fair number of gazes, but not enough to warrant scrutiny. Despite the cleanliness of the new world order, the warriors that made it possible were still alive and well. The elites viewed them as the unseen servants of progress, the reward of which was to continue breathing.

A quick scan uncovered Gate 42. The maiden pushed forward with a feigned disinterest, as though Orin was a bother and she had better places to be. She wandered up to a desk outside the gate. Behind it sat a stoic woman in a pressed suit. Two sentries stood behind her, guarding either side of the gangway. The maiden, having no idea what to expect, simply presented Orin like a floral bouquet.

"Sumus pluvia." *We are the rain*, Orin said.

The woman traded glances between them, then gestured to the gate.

The maiden added a groan to her nonchalance, then sauntered past the guards with Orin in her grasp. It seemed to work, as best she could tell. The guards paid her no mind as she entered the gangway. Halfway down, she released a laden breath.

"Latin?" she said.

"Yeah," Orin said. "Sala has a thing for ancient lit. He makes his lieutenants learn enough to converse."

"Servandum secreta." *Keeping secrets*, she said.

"Wow." Orin cocked an eyebrow. "A scholar and a killer."

"No. Just a very old lady."

As they neared the plane, another sentry revealed himself beside the entrance. But this one was different. No tactical gear, but mighty in stature with formal attire and a sheathed blade to his side. Apparently, the no-weapons policy only reached so far. His beefy frame completely blocked the doorway. Hard to maintain an air of disinterest when staring down a proper beast. Orin cleared his throat as the maiden strolled to a stop.

"Nos perducat procella." *We bring the storm*, Orin said with a rare deference.

The beast studied them for a moment, then grunted and stepped aside.

The maiden nodded her thanks and proceeded into the fuselage.

Once inside, the gutted cabin offered little to the eye. Crates and boxes were stacked to the ceiling, many crushed under their own weight. The entire space was dusty and disorganized, hardly the lair of a feared enforcer. A handful of workers tended to the mayhem. They rearranged boxes, hunted for files, and tossed the immaterial aside. The maiden sensed pity all around her, as the gift of life wasn't much gift at all.

"Head to the rear staircase," Orin said.

The maiden compiled and sidestepped various obstacles along the way. The workers ignored the intrusion, as the presence of Sala's minions had little impact on their duties. As the maiden neared the stairs, the dread inside Orin began to fester. She could sense the trembling, the panic, the despair of an unknown fate.

"Calm yourself," she said. "You get me in, I get you out. That's the deal, and I plan to honor it. I have no desire to end my path here."

Orin nodded and fought to steady his breathing. "His office is above us. Top of the stairs. Nothing left to do but climb."

The maiden maintained her stride as she entered the stairwell. She climbed to the top and stepped around a corner, bringing the full refuge into view. The room was spacious and free of clutter. Port windows were painted black. Several dark chests lined the walls. A pair of couches flanked a central desk about 20 feet away.

Behind the desk, a slender figure scribbled notes on a stack of papers. The top of his bald head faced the maiden. She cleared her throat, but the man did not respond. Instead, two hulking bodyguards rose from the couches. Their rugged garb and heavy boots conveyed a disinterest in peaceful negotiation. The maiden stepped forward, as did the guards. They met in the middle and came to a stop, placing a comfortable buffer between Sala and the maiden.

With a final stroke, Sala tossed his pen aside and leaned back in his chair. He briefly met eyes with the maiden, then shifted his attention to the unsightly package. "Orin," he said with minimal interest. "You seem less than yourself."

"Hardy har," Orin said mockingly.

"Must be some kind of story."

"We got ambushed."

"Kendra and Jamal?"

"Dead."

"Who hit you?"

"Funny story, we—" Orin screamed as the maiden ripped a chisel blade from his back, the one she had stitched into his flesh back at the cabin. In a single fluid motion, she dropped Orin, lunged to the right, and jammed the blade upwards through the bodyguard's chin. His muscles twitched as the chisel sliced through his brain. The other guard leapt into action. He swung at the maiden, who ducked both attempts before raking the blade across his knee. The guard yelped and crumpled to the floor, where she hammered the chisel into his ear. The crack of metal on bone brought a swift end to the encounter.

Orin writhed in pain as the maiden rose to her feet. The blade was soaked in blood and dripped down her fingers. She expected to find Sala cowering behind his desk, but her eyes deceived her. He hadn't moved at all. His placid demeanor remained intact as a smarmy grin crept across his face.

"I wondered when one of you would show up."

The maiden demurred. "One of."

"You're a Bone Maiden, yes?"

She did not respond, but the confusion was evident.

Sala gasped softly and leaned forward. "Could it be that the original ghost of the forest has graced me with her presence?" Rising to his feet, he stepped around the desk and moseyed up to the maiden without a shred of fear. He studied her closely, like a savant reviewing a piece of art. "Fascinating. The demon is real, yet powerless before me."

"One of," she said again.

"You started an uprising, my dear." Sala strolled around the maiden and returned to the desk. He pulled a finger across the surface, then leaned back and crossed his arms. "Brazil, Ghana, Moscow, Bone Maidens all over the world are threatening faction power. One of them managed to infiltrate the Russian Alliance. Killed seven agents before they took her down."

"And you think I'm here to do the same."

Sala chuckled. "Killing me won't stop the union, dear. You need Malin, and you need me to get close to him."

The maiden huffed and stepped forward.

Sala grinned, utterly confident in his assessment.

She settled in front of him and glanced away, as if to contemplate the impasse. "Many years ago, a little girl asked me to avenge her tribe. She was 12 years old and living in a survivor camp outside of New Orleans. A raiding party slaughtered her family and tried to rape her." Her eyes returned to Sala. "*Your* raiding party."

The grin faded from Sala's face.

The maiden grabbed his neck and plunged the blade into his heart. Sala barked with pain and fell back onto the desk, coughing and flailing. With a swift motion, she pulled the blade from his chest and sliced it across his neck, splattering blood on herself and the desk. She pinned him to the surface, then reached into the gash and ripped her prize from the flesh.

Sala pleaded for mercy as blood gurgled from his shredded throat.

The maiden lifted her crimson fist and held it over his face, painting his last worldly vision. "And now that promise is fulfilled." She then clasped his jaw beneath the chin and tore his head from the spine. The body went limp, forever sprawled atop the maple. The head bounced on the floor and rolled to a rest against the wall.

The maiden stood tall and loomed over the carnage. She unclenched her fist and opened her palm, revealing the ultimate prize. The hyoid bone glistened under a red sheen with bits of flesh still attached. She stared at it with a sudden detachment, as the great campaign had reached its logical end. She rubbed it between her fingertips, then let it drop to the floor. And with it, the moniker she embodied for decades.

"Don't mind me," Orin said from the floor behind her.

The maiden turned to find him facedown with an open wound in his back, exactly where she left him. Blood continued to trickle down his sides. He writhed in pain, but dared not howl. The bodyguards beside him had started crumbling into ash. She released a heavy sigh, then stepped over her battered partner.

"That was intense," he said through strained breaths. "Back hurts like a bitch, but I'm ready to get the hell out of here."

She knelt down and flipped him onto his back.

He swallowed a yelp as the wound pressed into the carpet. After a few pained grunts, he sighed with resolve and met eyes with the maiden. "I understand the play, I do. But that was a dick move. We need to talk about your—"

The maiden seized him by the throat and rose to her feet. He barked and squirmed as she stepped over to the desk. She shoved Sala's corpse to the floor, then slammed Orin onto the surface. He yawped on impact and wheezed beneath her grasp. The maiden towered over him, her hardened gaze piercing him like a hungry predator. She snatched the chisel and held it aloft, poised to hammer it into his flesh. His eyes widened as panic flooded his mind, for the maiden's true intent had finally revealed itself.

"You promised!" he said.

The maiden smirked. "I lied."

"But I helped you. You stand here because of *me*."

"One good deed does not erase decades of torment."

Orin whimpered. "I'm—I'm sorry. Please."

"So tell me, little piggy. What do you fear more than loss of power?"

His lips trembled as a single word crawled up his throat. "You."

The maiden grinned, then buried the blade into his eye socket. The chisel punched through his brain and out the back of his skull, embedding itself in the desk. Gasps turned to gurgles, then to nothing. She watched the life drain from the other eye, wholly unmoved by the sorrow.

And with a final twitch, the deed was done.

The maiden removed her hand from the chisel and left it there as a grim reminder, for no amount of power was untouchable. The flesh would dissolve around the blade and the notch it carved would remain. She glanced around the room one last time, taking stock of the oath she had honored.

An ashy haze floated through the room, infecting the air with finality. And so the maiden departed. She traced her steps down the stairs, through the cabin, and back to the entrance. The mighty guard stepped aside, allowing her to pass. As she did, she paused to meet his gaze.

"*Ego* perducat procella." *I bring the storm*, she said.

The guard recoiled slightly, then watched her amble up the gangway and vanish into the concourse. A sudden trepidation needled his bones, for the terror that lurked within would be revealed soon enough.

EPILOGUE

Two days later, the maiden was sitting quietly inside a wine bar. Her modest table rested against a tall window that overlooked the tarmac. She pulled her gaze across the planes, each carrying a different logo that unlocked a distant memory. Their destinations reached deep into her mind, uncovering sparks of pain and pleasure. She explored them all, the lives that were and the lives that could have been. But alive she was, and her mood was greatly enriched by a fourth glass of wine. An empty bottle sat on the table with a stumpy glass beside it. A small pool of red lingered inside, as if to savor the last moments of a perfect evening.

A faint orange glow had appeared in the distance, signaling the coming sunrise. The maiden watched it intensely as the muted rap of polite conversation filled the background. She caught a reflection of herself in the window. She loved the new sundress, its bold pattern as striking as it was comfortable. Her hair and skin were clean, glowing even. It took several washings, but the stench of retribution had finally faded.

The speech was good.

Despite his proclivity for bloodshed, Malin was oddly charismatic. A breath of fresh air for those attuned to suffering, but the maiden knew better. She understood him as a crafty broker, a leech of power destined to fall. But even so, the union had been announced. The cartel would join the Northwestern States, and they in turn would join the global alliance.

NExUS, they called it.

A global tyranny disguised as a public service.

But then again, anything was better than the current misery.

The Bone Maiden, having birthed a rebellion that demanded justice, would now reap the fruits of its ashes. But peace was peace, and the means gain merit when life is barely worth living. The Great Onslaught was a festering wound, a lingering noose, and the world was desperate to wake from the nightmare. Perhaps a union was inevitable, but only the callous march of time would reveal its worth.

A waitress wandered by and stopped to check on the maiden. "Is there anything else I can get for you?" she asked with a pleasant tone.

"No, that's okay." The maiden downed the last sip and relinquished the glass. "Thank you, though. And I must say, that is fine Bordeaux."

"It's my favorite too," the waitress said. She winked, then added the glass to her tray. "We should get another shipment in soon if you fancy a return."

"Count on it." The maiden returned the wink, then plucked the cork from the empty bottle before it whisked away. She gave it a hearty sniff and released a moan of pleasure. "Mind if I keep this?"

"Certainly."

The maiden smiled, then reached into her new satchel. A leatherbound journal was tucked inside. The pages were fresh and smelled of renewal. She had obtained it from a book stand not hours earlier, along with a handful of classic tales that she yearned to read through a newfound lens. She pushed them aside and tucked the cork into a pocket.

"Thank you, miss ..." The maiden extended her hand.

"Jessica," the woman said politely, then completed the shake.

"Nice to meet you, Jessica. I'm Elizabeth."

ZACHRY WHEELER

THE END

The story continues with:
Transient (Immortal Wake #1)

ABOUT THE AUTHOR

Zachry Wheeler is an award-winning science fiction author. His many interests include photon hunting, full-contact chess, and vertical wit. He lives on Earth with his wife and cats.

Learn more at **ZachryWheeler.com**

If you enjoyed this harrowing tale, please consider posting a short review. Ratings and reviews are the currency by which authors gain visibility. They are the single greatest way to show your support and keep us writing the stories you love.

Thank you for reading!